For Jacobo, Paloma, Segismon, Julia and little Pepe

Bloomsbury Publishing, London, New Delhi, New York and Sydney

First published in Great Britain in 2008 by Bloomsbury Publishing Plc
50 Bedford Square, London, WC1B 3DP

This edition first published in Great Britain in 2014

A CIP catalogue record of this book is available from the British Library

ISBN 978 1 4088 5002 2 (PB)
ISBN 978 1 4088 3897 6 (eBook)
Printed in China by C&C Offset Printing Co Ltd, Shenzhen, Guangdong

1 3 5 7 9 10 8 6 4 2

All papers used by Bloomsbury Publishing are natural, recyclable products
made from wood grown in well-managed forests.
The manufacturing processes conform to the environmental regulations of the country of origin

www.bloomsbury.com

Marvin Gets MAD!

Joseph Theobald

BLOOMSBURY

LONDON NEW DELHI NEW YORK SYDNEY

One perfect morning Marvin and Molly
found a tree full of big, juicy apples.

There was one apple that Marvin really wanted but no matter how high he jumped, he couldn't quite reach it.

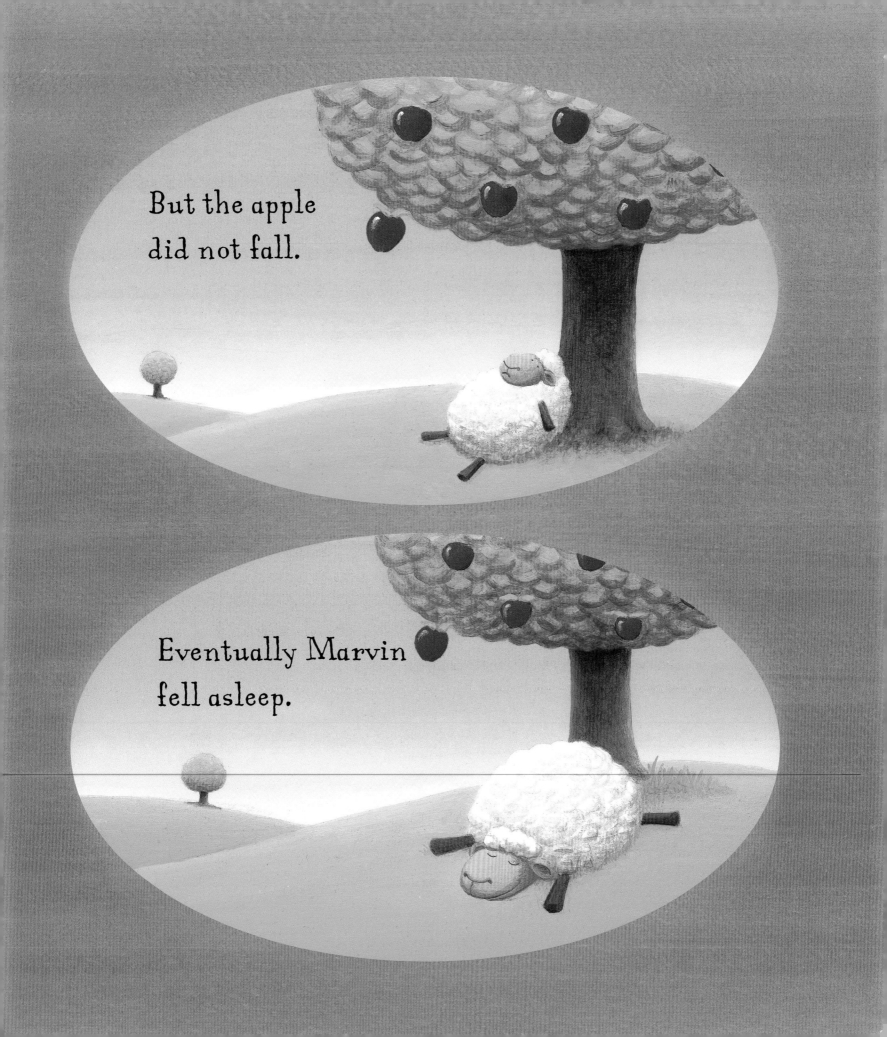

But the apple did not fall.

Eventually Marvin fell asleep.

When Marvin woke up, the apple was gone.
Molly was eating it!

"I wanted that apple!" shouted Marvin.
"Sorry," said Molly. "I didn't know."

Marvin was not happy.

"Don't get mad with me," said Molly.
"There are lots more apples in the tree."

"I WANTED THAT APPLE!" shouted Marvin.

"AND YOU'VE EATEN IT!!"

Marvin was so mad . . . he grew
MAD teeth, **MAD** horns,
MAD feet, and a **MAD** tail.

"I WANT

MY APPLE!!"

"Calm down," said Molly.

"NO!" shouted Marvin, and he stamped on the flowers,

he knocked over the chicken shed,

Marvin
Gets
MAD!

Joseph Theobald

BLOOMSBURY

he frightened the ducks,

and bit a cow's tail.

Marvin didn't know what he wanted any more.
He stamped his big mad feet and let out a big mad . . .

As Marvin stamped harder and harder,
the ground began to rumble underneath him . . .
And suddenly . . .

The ground opened
up and swallowed him
whole.

Marvin fell deeper and
deeper and
landed with a thud,
all alone in the dark.

"BAAAA!" shouted
Marvin,
but no one could hear him.

He tried to break the wall,
but that only hurt his head.

Marvin was all alone.

He closed his eyes and remembered
the perfect day in the meadow.
I wish Molly was here, he thought.
Gradually Marvin felt less mad.

When Marvin opened his eyes, there was Molly!
"I'm sorry I was so angry," said Marvin.
"That's OK," said Molly. "I came to find you.
I thought you might be lost. And look, I've found
another big, juicy apple. It's for you!"

"Thank you!" said Marvin.
And Molly showed Marvin
the way back up to the meadow.

Everything was perfect again.
But Marvin didn't want an apple any more . . .
He wanted a **pear!**

But no matter how high he jumped,
he couldn't quite reach it.